For Toby and Emma, with oodles of love A.B.

For Lucy and Harry S.W.

First published in Great Britain in 2010 by
Piccadilly Press Ltd, 5 Castle Road, London NW1 8PR
www.piccadillypress.co.uk

Text © Abi Burlingham, 2010
Illustrations copyright © Sarah Warburton, 2010

Designed by Simon Davis
Printed and bound in China by WKT
Colour reproduction by Dot Gradations

ISBN: 978 1 84812 035 8 (hardback)
978 1 84812 034 1 (paperback)

1 3 5 7 9 10 8 6 4 2

Ruby and Grub

Abi Burlingham
Illustrated by Sarah Warburton

PICCADILLY PRESS • LONDON

This is me,
I'm Ruby.

This is Grub,
he's a grubby, mucky pup!

Grub loves to dig.

He digs and digs and digs.

When I shout,

"Stop digging!"

he doesn't stop digging.

Do you know what he does?

He carries on digging.

I don't think he can hear me.

Sometimes he turns on his side,
like this.
I say, "No, Grub, no!"
But he doesn't listen.

I say, "Walk, Grub, walk!"

Do you know what he does?

He rolls on his other side!

I think Grub's tired.

Sometimes,
Grub rolls over and over **SO** much
that he needs a bath.

I say, "In, Grub, in!"
Do you know what he does?
He leaps in the bath,
then he rolls over and over
IN THE BATH!

I say, "Oh no, Grub!"

Then I am wet too.

I look like **I'VE** had a bath!

I think Grub thinks it's funny.

It **is** quite funny.

Last week I had a bad tummy.
Grub sat by my bed
and wouldn't move –
ALL DAY!
"Bed, Grub!" I said.
Do you know what he did?
He sat on **MY** bed.
I think he thought it was **HIS** bed.

Then one day,
something **TERRIBLE** happened.
Grub got out!

Do you know what he did?
He chased the ice-cream van down the street
and the van had to stop.

I told him, "Grub, that's bad!
But then I thought,
"No, it's good,"
and I bought some ice-cream.

It was delicious!
Grub thought so too.

Then one day, something **EVEN MORE TERRIBLE** happened.

Grub dug a hole under our fence,

and under next door's fence.

It took six people to catch him and bring him back.

Mum wasn't pleased ONE BIT!
"THAT IS IT!" she said, "I've had enough!
Grub, you are just TOO naughty, TOO mucky
and TOO much trouble," she said.
"Grub, you will have to GO!"

I cried,
but Mum
wouldn't
budge.

So we took him to Uncle Tom's.

Uncle Tom had three dogs already.

He didn't mind one more.

Grub raced out the house to see us.

Do you know what he did?

He ran around in circles.

He rolled in the mud.

He covered me in muddy paw prints.

"He's naughty, he's mucky
and he's far too much trouble," said Mum.
"But we just miss him TOO much."

"Please can he come home?" I asked Uncle Tom.
Uncle Tom didn't mind one bit.
He has three dogs already.

I have Grub,
and Grub has me!